# #1 ADVENTURES OF CHARLIE
## A 6TH GRADE GAMER

WRITTEN BY
# CONNOR GRAYSON

# A NOTE FROM
# CONNOR GRAYSON ☆

This series is a love letter to my 11-year-old gamer self, who was reluctant to pick up a book. I'm especially proud of the audiobooks. **They're so much fun!**

They're also game changing for reluctant readers. I'm a huge fan of the read along.

The book + audiobook combo helps alleviate common barriers to reading and instill confidence and excitement in young gamers.

*The Adventures of Charlie: A 6th Grade Gamer #1 audiobook is **FREE** to Insider's Club members.*

**FREE AUDIOBOOK!**
JOIN THE INSIDER'S CLUB →
*FREE FOR CURRENT MEMBERS TOO

CONNORGRAYSON.COM

# GAME
# OVER

I swear she's trying to sabotage me.

"You really don't want me to win, do you?" I ask, not taking my eyes off the screen.

"Charlie, what are you talking about?"

"Mom, you're trying to sabotage me. Stop breathing so loud!"

She says something else, but it sounds like *wah wah wah*.

1

Zoning into the dungeon, I wonder if I'm dead. The controller slips in my hand and I squeeze it hard.

Not like I'm a ghost dead, but like ghosts are floating everywhere and I'll die dead.

A black mist crawls over my feet and up my legs. It wraps around me like a snake, and chills creep up my spine. I'm so cold my head feels like an ice block.

Crouched in a narrow hall outside a game room, I peek inside. It's dark, but bright from the glow of ghosts. The floor is checkered stone like a chessboard and splattered in dirt. Two green felt tables remind me of Grandpa's playing card table. One is stuffed full of half-painted figurines. Board games litter the other. Seven ghosts hover around each table, slumped like big-glowing-blobs-of-lazy.

A breeze whips dust in the air. I cough and quickly cover my mouth, hoping the mobs didn't hear me. My tongue snakes around the inside of my mouth and over my teeth. It feels gritty and tastes like dirt. Take a bite, feel it crunch.

Drag your feet two steps forward and peer around the corner to the right. It's so dark you have to squint, but the coast is clear. Glancing left, it's the same. Which way to go?

Hugging the wall, I turn the corner and slide through the dark. My brain screams to stay close. Keep your hand on the wall, feel how it's rough like concrete.

What's the worst that can happen? A ghost spots me, shrieks, then attacks? It only stings when you die. In most games you respawn at the beginning of the level, but not here. Here everything changes. You start over. New level. No saves. You need to be the best to win.

It's all a matter of finding the secret. Every video game has a secret to winning. There's an item to find, or a puzzle to solve, and boom, you're one step away from victory.

Halfway across the room is an unlit torch high on the wall, attached with a big metal ring. Maybe too high. Hmm. I slip like a ninja down the wall until I'm right below my target. A flapping sound reminds me of the curtains at night when my window is open. I freeze and glance around. A ghost is two feet away. Staring right at me. My eyes snap shut and my body shakes. I squeeze a fist hard enough fingernails dig into my hands. Just. Don't. Move.

The flapping fades to nothing.

I crack an eye open. The ghost vanished. Whew.

The torch is right above me. Even standing on my tip-toes my fingers touch nothing but air. I jump and smack the bottom of the thing. Metal scratches stone for a quick second. It's moving!

Spotting a wooden crate a few feet away, a light bulb goes off. But it's surrounded by monsters. Ugh.

I'll risk it.

I ninja sneak up to the box, grab hold and drag it towards the wall. The ghosts notice me, then look away not seeming to care.

You know what happens next right?

First, I maneuver the crate and climb it like a ladder. Then I reach up, grasp the torch, and twist the ring. Metal grinds along the wall for a half-turn and stops with a loud click-clunk.

I twist around as the far wall crumbles to pieces. Lights stream through the cracks. Yes!

Hopping down, I hesitate and scan the room. My stomach flips.

Something's wrong.

The room is no longer stuffed with big-glowing-blobs-of-lazy.

Very, very wrong.

It's jammed with snarling, shrieking ghosts and they're all flying towards me.

"Turn off the video game. I need to tell you something," Mom says as she steps in front of me.

I wave her away and crane my neck. "Mom, move!"

"It's important, Charlie."

"You're making me die! Move!"

She reaches down and rips the cord out of the wall. I watch in horror as the screen goes black.

# WIZARD'S DELIVERY
★

When Mom told me we had to move, I told her no. No way. She said we'd buy a Nintendo Switch when we got there. My exact words were something like, "When do we leave?"

It took a week to fill all the boxes. Dad stuffed his U-Haul with most of them. He took the video game consoles and all my games. *It'll be okay, you're getting a Switch,* he said. *Your saves are in the cloud.* You're right,

Dad. *None of this is your fault, you know. Things are different now.* Thanks, Dad.

I don't know.

Mom told me it's okay because we're minimalists. Whatever that means. A bed, our clothes, and a couple boxes filled one corner of our U-Haul. She asked me to keep our precious cargo up front in the cab. Her new gold pen and journals, our blender (she calls me a blender ninja), and the scrapbook she made me. It's full of pictures I'd rather not exist. The ones where you're a naked baby covered in spaghetti, or doing something dumb like washing your hands in the toilet. It's embarrassing.

At least we'll still be able to make smoothies together. It's one of my favorite things because it's one of Mom's favorite things. She makes me chop everything before throwing it into the blender. Who knows why. When I asked her once, she said, *Charlie, you're twelve, you need knife skills.*

She's kinda weird.

For one of her concoctions, you have to chop onions. She calls them shallots. I don't know. You wear swim goggles, otherwise your eyes water so much you cry like a baby.

So you chop up two shallots and toss them in the blender. She'll cram in handfuls of nasty green stuff.

Then you slice up an apple, making sure all the pieces are the same size. *Be precise,* she'll say, *it matters.*

Next, a dollop of peanut butter goes in. You sneak in extra. She tops it off with milk. Usually a weird one like oat milk. Who the heck makes milk out of oatmeal? I don't get it.

Finally, you snap the lid down and flip the switch on. The blender spins, screams, and rattles the whole counter. The secret is to let it go exactly sixty-seven seconds then flip the switch off.

Mom will pour us each a full jar—it's bright green with swirls of peanut butter running around. It smells a little like grass and a lot like sunshine. Might as well call it Goblin Grub.

After the first big suck on the straw, she dances and sings about making magic. She's so weird it makes me laugh.

Dad always said the whole "smoothie thing" is crazy and not worth the mess. He never even tried it.

He asked if I wanted to have any friends over tonight, our last night, for pizza. *We can play video games one last time. Any game,* he said. *Even the ones your mom doesn't like.*

I told him no. No thanks, Dad. I'm excited to get going so I can get my Switch. I need to sleep so tomorrow will come. The truth, though, is that I've never been good at making friends. And we're leaving anyway, so what does it matter.

Mom just told me to put the big jugs of Dad's pennies in our U-Haul. Ten massive five-gallon jugs. You've seen them, they're kinda see-through blue.

"Why? What in the world do we need those for? They weigh like a million pounds."

"That's how you buy your video game. Count enough pennies, and we'll take them to the bank, then—"

"Are you kidding me? That will take forever—you promised!"

"That's the deal. There's more to life than video games, Charlie. You'll find something else to—"

I walk away. I move the stupid jugs of pennies, but all I can think about are liars. I hate liars. And both Mom and Dad are liars.

Yanking the U-Haul door open, there's a scuttering sound. It's coming from the shadows under the seat. Maybe a monster, probably a squirrel. Squinting to see, it's nothing but an old candy wrapper. Something blows past my face and then there's a bang behind me. Twisting around, I spot a new dent in the door, brushing it with a finger the metal feels cold and slippery like it's covered in slime. Weird.

Plopping into the seat, something crunches. Ugh. I yank it out from under my butt. It's an old shoe box wrapped with sticky green string. There's a note attached.

*Enclosed: Wizard Eyes. They're yours now. Shh. We'll talk soon.*

I read it again so hard my forehead crinkles. I don't know.

Mom hops into the driver's seat and slams the door. I crush the note in my hand, not wanting her to see it. I'm not sure why. She starts the truck and looks at me.

"What's in the box?"

What is in the box? What, exactly, are Wizard Eyes? And who gave them to me? I unzip my backpack and shuffle around Goblin Grub ingredients to make room, then stuff the shoe box in.

"Nothing," I say. "It's nothing."

**FREE AUDIOBOOK!**
JOIN THE INSIDER'S CLUB
*FREE FOR CURRENT MEMBERS TOO

CONNORGRAYSON.COM

# MY WIZARD
# EYES

Driving to Arizona is super-boring. It's a huge desert, and there's nothing to see but dirt and old cacti that people shoot holes in with shotguns.

I don't know.

We have lunch at a rest stop. Cheese sandwich for me, and salad for Mom. Kicking my backpack, the top flops open, staring me in the face is the shoe box. Hmm.

What do you think is inside? I glance at Mom, and she just raises her eyebrows and asks me what it is.

"I have to pee," I say, grabbing my backpack and hopping out of the truck.

The bathroom is gross, there's one empty stall without something nasty all over the seat. Are there actual eyeballs in the shoe box? I don't know. It'd be disgusting if there were. Last year in science class, the town vet showed us how to dissect cow eyes. He brought in a big Mason jar full of them—cow eyeballs, seriously.

It's a lot harder to slice into an eyeball than you think. Press the knife down too fast, the eye slips out and rolls across the table like a slimy ping pong ball. You're lucky to catch it before it slips and slides halfway across the room.

I lock the door and sit down. The seat is warm, don't think about it. I wrestle the shoe box out of my backpack and start unwrapping all the green string. And keep unwrapping for, like, ever. It's a never-ending story. The string rolls into a ball easily, because it's waxy, like floss, and sticky. By the time I'm done, it's the size of a softball: a monster snot wad. I stuff it so far down in my backpack you'll need to dig to pick it out.

Cracking the box open, I discover a pair of high-tech-looking goggles. No slimy eyeballs. The goggles are a mix of silver and gold metal. They kinda look like jet engines you wear on your face. With round, blue, mirrored lenses and a dark-colored head-strap. Almost like my onion-chopping goggles. If my onion-chopping ones were cool.

I try putting them on, but they're way too big. They just slip down my face. Searching for strap adjustments, I run my finger around the lenses when words appear out of nowhere: *Tap here four times to resize.* The period at the end of the sentence pulsates and glows. Weird. A button? Hmm.

BANG!

"Are you done in there yet? I have to go," says someone, banging on the door to my bathroom stall.

"Use another one," I say, shaking my head.

"Kid, they got crap everywhere. Hurry up!"

I cradle the Wizard Eyes in my hand and look closer. Maybe it's like invisible ink until you touch the button. Or if you rub it enough with your finger, a genie pops out to grant you a wish. I rub it until the metal feels hot. Nothing. Okay, no genie.

I slip the goggles back on, careful to hold the strap in the right spot. Then tap the button. Four times. Something clicks, and the strap tightens like a rubber band when you pull it between two fingers.

BANG! BANG!

"Kid, hurry. This is an emergency!"

"Use another one, okay," I say, swiveling my head around to see if anything appears different through the Wizard Eyes. They are super-light, like feathers on my face. Why are they even called Wizard Eyes? I don't know.

RATTLE! RATTLE!

The door shakes so much I worry it will pop open. I slam a hand on it to hold it closed, keeping my fingers on the lock. This weirdo isn't walking in on me.

"There isn't another one. Hurry, or I'll bust the lock."

"Dude, seriously," I say.

Wondering what will happen if I touch the other side of the goggles... tap, tap. Nothing. Tap, tap, tap times two, and the inside of the goggles glow a lime-green color.

A tiny red arrow appears and drifts to the right until it's slowly bouncing on the edge of the goggles. I drop the lock and turn around. The red arrow floats across my vision and bumps into the other side of the goggles. Is it pointing at something specific? Like a compass?

"What the..." I say out loud.

"Kid. You've got the Eyes on now. I'm coming in. You better have your pants up."

Wait, what?

The lock clicks and the stall door creaks until... SLAM! A gust of wind smelling like chocolate-covered fish guts attacks me. Ugh. Gag. I stumble back and end up sitting on the toilet seat. It's still warm, don't think about it.

It isn't a guy standing there grinning at me. It's a rat. An insanely tall rat with a potbelly and five horns. He's rubbing the longest one, and it squeaks like a violin. And he's dead, the way ghosts are dead. It's a dead horned rat.

"No, I'm not Splinter. Everyone asks. Get my note? Yeah, you did," the dead horned rat says.

"AHH!" I scramble back as far as possible and land on top of the toilet.

The rat-man glances side to side and then closes the stall door. "Shh, quiet. It's cool," he says, gesturing with clawed hands. "I've got a deal for you, Charlie. And, oh man, you'll like it. You'll like it so much more than counting pennies all summer. Oh man, are you excited?"

"Who—what—who are you?" I say.

Then he takes a rolled piece of paper out of a pocket and offers it to me. "Just a harbinger. Read this and check the list. Bring the things on it when you come," he says. Pointing at the goggles, "The Wizard Eyes will show you where to go."

# THE DEAD HORNED RAT

 **MAGIC ATTACK** | **MELEE ATTACK**

## STENCH

THE RAT-MAN WILL
LET LOOSE A STENCH
SO DISGUSTING
IT'LL STUN YOU.
BECAUSE WHILE YOU'RE
IN LA-LA-LAND HE'LL
HIT YOU WITH TAIL WHIP!

## TAIL WHIP

THE RAT-MAN WILL
TWIST AWAY FROM AN
ENEMY, DRAWING THEM
IN CLOSER, THEN
EXPLODE TOWARDS
THEM, WHIPPING HIS TAIL
LIKE A NINJA STRIKE!

# STOLEN
# THING

The list. You're wondering about the list. It only took two days, and a lot of cereal, to find everything except the last item.

I don't know.

Our new home looks like a house, but it's a trailer with a porch wrapping around like a half-moon and a five-foot-tall, floppy pool, down a small hill, in the front yard.

When I first see her, I think she'll stop at the pool. It's the green polka-dot floaties hugging her arms that make me think it. But she flies right by.

She bears down on the handlebars and pumps her legs hard, backpack swinging from side to side as she zooms up the hill towards me. Her long skirt flaps and snaps as it's whipped by the wind. It'll get sucked into the spokes, and she'll flip and face plant.

I wipe sweat from my forehead and rub my hand on my jeans. Mom and I came here two days ago, and it's all right. I guess. It's quiet, not like the city. Mom's finally finishing her book. It's something about gold.

I don't know.

There's a broken TV and a couple Percy Jackson books, but that's about it. No video games, which is so terrible I might die. Oh, and a million pennies to count before buying my Switch.

The girl skids to a stop about two-and-a-half inches from the edge of the porch.

"The pool is always empty, you know?" she says, taking off her glasses and wiping along each side of her nose with two fingers.

"Why are you wearing pool floaties?" I ask, picking up a tiny paper sleeve and dropping pennies in.

"Why are you doing that?" She puts her glasses back on and they sit crooked.

"So I can buy a Switch," I say, closing the top of a roll of pennies.

She rolls her eyes and says, "You're a gamer?"

"You aren't?"

"I play my mom's old Nintendo sometimes. I love using the secret code to get extra lives," she says.

"What secret code?"

"I made it a song so I could remember," she says, jumping off the bike and letting it crash to the ground.

"Up, up, down, down go ahead, skip around," she sings, skipping in a circle. "Left, right, left, right, monsters come out at midnight."

I snort and shake my head. "What are you doing?"

"Skipping like a bunny," she says.

I don't know.

"Bunnies don't skip, they hop," I say. Getting up, I hop in a circle. "Like this."

The back of my neck prickles. She's watching, isn't she? My face gets hot and my heart thumps like crazy. Skidding to a stop, I face her. She cocks her head to the side, and looks confused, like she's never seen someone hop before.

"What?" I say.

"Have you been to the top of that mountain yet? It's haunted, you know," she says, pointing to the mountain behind our trailer.

"Haunted like ghosts and stuff?"

"Like a ghost and stuff. The ugly unicorn lives up there." She yanks two bunches of her long hair straight above her head. "She has a bunch of horns like this."

"Unicorns have one—" I say, but she cuts me off.

"Hello? I said *ugly* unicorn," she says, swinging her backpack off and letting it clunk on the porch. A pair of Wizard Eyes tumble onto the deck.

"Hey—where'd you get those?" I ask, pointing at the pair of goggles identical to mine from the dead horned rat.

"The ugly unicorn. That's how I found the mountain house," she says, picking up the Wizard Eyes. "They have this arrow—"

"An arrow that spins and bounces on the inside when you turn? Like it's pointing at something?"

"How do you know?" she asks, balancing the goggles on her face.

"Don't you know how to make them fit? Watch." I reach into my backpack and pull out my Wizard Eyes. Pressing them to my face, I tap on the side four times, and the strap tightens. She mimics me, and the straps of her Wizard Eyes resize just like mine.

"Thanks! I'm Evie. And you should know, I don't believe in Santa Claus, but I believe in ghosts." She crosses her arms across her chest and glares right at me. I feel nervous, like I do right before my mom yells.

I don't know.

"Uh, hi. I'm Charlie and..." I rub my neck and try to not look right at her. "Yeah, me too."

"So you met the ugly unicorn then?"

"No, some dead rat-man with five horns. He told me the Wizard Eyes would show me where to go and gave me this." I reach into my bag to grab the paper from the dead horned rat.

"The game rules and what to bring?" She asks.

"Do you really think we'll get *anything* we want if we win? Like anything?" I ask, looking at the list again. I don't know if I can do it.

Evie shrugs her shoulders and tilts her head. "One way to find out. I have everything on the list and I'm going to the mountain house. Do you want to go with me? That's where the Wizard Eyes are telling us to go."

She raises her eyebrows at me. Hmm. Should I do it? It's only one more thing on my list. My heart beats faster. I'd be playing a game, and if I win, I get anything I want. My hands are sweaty. The letter said it would be like a real-life video game.

"I'll be right back," I say, snatching up my backpack and going inside.

Searching around, I don't see Mom. I call for her, and she yells back from the bathroom. "I'm going to play with a new friend. I'll be back soon," I say. My chest is on fire. Sitting on the desk is Mom's new gold pen. She loves it and keeps saying how it's our portal to safety. An elephant is sitting on my chest, I can barely breathe. The last thing on the list must be special. My legs are rubber. I snatch the pen and stuff it in my pocket.

It said to steal it.

# HILL
# HOUSE

There's nothing on the top of the mountain except a grassy clearing surrounded by a bunch of cracked boulders, a handful of rotting trees and cacti, and a rusted iron fence with a broken gate lying on the ground.

"Where's the house?" I ask Evie.

She's wearing her Wizard Eyes, searching the sky. Her fingers are tracing some shape from point to point.

"What are you doing?" I ask, following her gaze. The

sky is blue with a handful of wispy clouds moving in slow-mo.

"Counting stars in the shape of a star," she says.

"Stars? It's the middle of the day, there are no stars," I say.

"Put on your goggles. It's always night here with the Wizard Eyes," she says, waving at the iron gate.

I don't know.

I fasten on my Wizard Eyes, and she's right. It's super-dark, and the sky's packed with big, bulging clouds that look mean. Like they'll fling knives of rain at us. I shiver.

Evie sprints away and I see who—or what—she was waving at. The ugly unicorn. Sure enough, there are a bunch of horns where there should be one. And the unicorn only has three legs.

I take a step to follow when I hear *him* behind me.

"You made it," he says.

I spin around and see the dead horned rat. He's holding a bowl. Things in the bowl squirm. They're not Cheerios.

"What is this place?" I ask, eyeing the bowl.

He plucks a thing from the bowl and pops it into his mouth. He chews and offers the bowl to me. "Want one?" he asks. A spider scurries out of his ghost-face and crawls into his ear. "So annoying when they do that."

"Yuck," I say, trying not to puke.

"This is the House on the Hill. Home of the Seven. Sanctuary of Seven Keys. The place where dreams come true," the rat-man says with a flick of his tail and a flourish of his hand. "If you win, that is."

"What house?" I say, glancing around the empty clearing.

"Ah yes, the house. The house is late. It will be here soon. Patience. Do you have the items from the list?"

"The letter said I get magical powers?" I ask.

"You do. Make the deal, go inside the house and choose your powers," he says, stepping towards the fallen iron gate. "The items?"

I rummage through my backpack until I find the plastic bag with my items. I hand it over to the rat-man. He peers into the bag. "Three hearts, a star, and a red balloon. Never expected marshmallows. Luckily, I wasn't specific. How much cereal did you eat?" he says, pouring my items into his bowl of bugs. "Nevermind. The last item?"

I wipe my hand on my jeans and pull Mom's gold pen from my pocket. "Do I get it back?"

"Unlikely, but I never say never," the rat-man says, swiping the pen from my hand.

Evie runs up. "Are you going in? I'm going in. I turned in my items."

The ground rumbles and wobbles. Wind whips through the tall grass, puffing up the smell of rotten eggs. Two massive black bird feet lunge over the boulders and smash into the ground, leaving T-Rex sized impressions.

On top of the bird legs is a house, an old cranky house with not enough windows and too many doors. It struts towards the fallen iron gate and stops just before.

"Hello, old friend," the dead horned rat yells. "You're late!"

The bird-house plops down with a sigh, and the legs disappear. Leaving an old house gawking at me. Its doors flap and groan in the breeze. Things crawl out of the ground and creep in its shadow.

Something rushes through the grass to my right, darting towards the house. I freeze.

"What was that?"

"Probably a jelly," Evie says, skipping ahead through the grass. "There are lots of them here. They have fat legs and are kinda melty."

The grass waves wildly as more invisible bodies dart through close to the ground. One bounces off my leg, covering me in slimy goop. "Hey—gross!" It sprints off before I can see it.

Behind me, the ground crunches under shuffling feet. Lots of feet. Glancing back, the field overflows with scarecrows wearing sad faces. Floppy hats cover their eyes, and backpacks bulging with stone slow them down.

"What are those?" I ask.

"Workers. Players past. They don't matter," the dead horned rat says, stepping up to the door of the house and standing next to Evie, who's waiting.

"Who cares? Let's go!" Evie says.

"Tell me again," I say to the rat-man.

"You walk through the door, you accept the deal. You get magic powers to battle monsters, solve puzzles, discover items and treasure. Think of it as playing the latest video game. The Seven carry keys. Get a key, open a door. Get all—"

"And when I win, I get anything I want? One magic wish?"

"Yes. When you win. But you cannot leave the house until you do," he says. Turning to both Evie and me, he asks, "Do you want to play?"

"I do," Evie says as she disappears through the door.

The dead horned rat plucks a worm from his bowl and slurps it up like a noodle. "You don't even have to count pennies to play," he says, walking through the door.

I'm just trying to live my best life. And I can't do that sitting on a porch counting pennies forever. I can do this. I can win. Right?

"Charlie, you've got to see this!" Evie yells from inside.

It's my decision to make. I choose and bolt through the door. "What? What is it?"

Evie is bouncing on her toes with a huge grin on her face. A goblin is standing next to her.

"Noob, can you take longer? Stump is waiting," the goblin says.

I widen my eyes and glance at Evie. She's bobbing her head so hard I think it's about to snap off. "It's Grrblin. Grrblin the goblin!"

"If you laugh, I'll kill you before a boss mob ever has the chance. Let's go," Grrblin says.

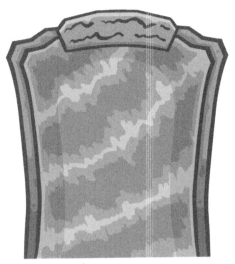

# GOING
# INSIDE
## ※

I follow Grrblin, Evie, and the dead horned rat down a long, dark hallway. It stinks like sour milk and reminds me of Sirius Black's house.

"Who's the goblin?" I whisper to the rat-man.

"He's your group leader. He'll teach you a lot. How many room runs do you have under your belt now, Grrblin?" he asks.

Grrblin makes a growling noise. "Too many."

"What do you mean 'group'?" I ask. "I thought this was a video game thing."

"It's like a video game thing," the rat-man says, waving his hand around like so-so. "One you play with others."

"I can do it myself. I always do."

"Maybe that's your problem."

I have no idea what he's talking about. What problem? I don't have a problem with beating video games. It's kinda my thing.

We reach the end of the hall, and there's a shimmering door. Above the door is a puppet with no legs hanging by strings. There's a message written on its chest.

*One Person At A Time. NO Exceptions!*

I don't know.

"Evie, Charlie. This is the chance to change your mind. I'll go first. Grrblin next. You each go, if you want to continue. Once you cross over, you're committed. It's no shame if you're scared and want to turn around. Don't cross together. I can't undo what happens," he says, stepping through and disappearing.

I try to see what's on the other side of the shimmer, but everything looks like static electricity. It reminds me of an old TV.

"If you're scared," Grrblin spits, then jumps through.

"Why not twos? Turns you into a melty-jelly mutant person, I bet," Evie says as she crosses.

I'm alone in the hallway.

The rat-man is right. I am scared, at least a little, and unsure. It's all so weird. What am I doing? I turn around and see light outside. Mom's probably wondering where I am. She won't be mad about the pen, not if I explain. I could run, get out. Nobody will stop me. I can finish counting pennies, get my Switch, and pretend I never found the Wizard Eyes.

But I'd never win the one wish. What I want I can't get by counting pennies.

I inspect the shimmer. It looks red, but it's blue. I reach out my fingertips and energy lights my palm like a rainbow and runs up my arm. I feel tingly, and goosebumps sprout all over.

Pressing my entire body through, for a split second, I'm floating in space.

# THE SCARECROW

 **MAGIC ATTACK** | **MELEE ATTACK**

## SAD SCREAM

THE SCARECROW MIGHT BELT OUT A SAD SCREAM SO TERRIBLE AND DEPRESSING YOU'LL FALL ASLEEP ON THE SPOT. IF YOU'RE NOT CAREFUL, YOU MAY WAKE UP WITH A SACK OF STONES ON YOUR BACK!

## ROCK THROW

THE SCARECROWS WERE PLAYERS, BEFORE THEY GAVE UP! THEY'LL WHIP A STONE BRICK AT YOUR FACE IF YOU CROSS THEM. THEIR LONG ARMS LAUNCH THE BRICK LIKE A MISSILE. GOOD LUCK DODGING IT!

# THE
# FATES

We're crowded together in the center of a room bigger than my school's gym. Half the room is jam-packed with long tables smothered in everything from burgers and tacos to fruits and veggies. No one sits at the tables. A few kids are inspecting food. They're all wearing Wizard Eyes.

One girl picks up an apple. I think it's an apple. It's half-eaten and dripping black. She sniffs and wrinkles her nose like it's rotten. Spinning the apple in her hand, she studies it with the Wizard Eyes. Then she takes a bite! Her cheeks puff out, and she spazzes for a second like she'll puke, then chokes it down.

She lifts her hand and flexes her fingers into the shape of a claw. Then she squeezes them into a fist. Tight enough her knuckles turn white. When she flings her fingers open a fireball appears and hovers above her hand. She cackles like a witch. "Yeeeesssss!"

One table is lined with machines and big bottles of glowing goop. I crane to see better, and the machines all look like my blender! One kid throws ingredients into a blender. Taps buttons, and the machine turns on, spins, screams, and rattles the entire table. They're making smoothies. Another girl pours a concoction into a big red cup, filling it with bright-orange slushy. I swear she glows as she drinks.

RIZZZZZ! RIZZZZZZ! RIZZZZZ!

Turning I see kids crawling along walls on the other side of the room. Drilling holes.

I don't know.

One kid drills a hole, squeezes his eyeball right up to it, and starts yelling. "Blue room. Ghosts. Puzzle, maybe? The walls keep moving."

Another kid squishes her face to the wall and starts yelling. "Key mob. I have a key mob."

Everyone freezes, their heads snap up, and they stare

at the girl who cried key mob. The tallest boy I've ever seen rushes up with a rolling white board. Tall boy frantically quizzes the girl, scribbling her answers on the board as fast as he can.

"What are they doing?" I ask.

"Watching instead of playing. It's dumb, don't do it," Grrblin says from behind me.

I turn around. Grrblin stands peering at me. He's wearing an old leather pack. Like mine, but it's totally different. Tubes covered in living vines run over his shoulders and down his arms from the pack. Protecting his wrists and covering the tops of his hands are silver skeleton bones.

"Watching what?" Evie asks, as she scoots up next to me.

"Looking for trends, patterns. See the tall kid? He's been here the longest but hasn't run a room in ages. He thinks he'll figure out how the rooms spawn, then he can just go after the key mobs."

The goblin snaps a button on his pack. A baseball-sized thing whizzes down one tube. He snags it just in time and tosses it hand to hand. I realize it's a mass of weeds and vines writhing and curling around his fingers.

"You keep saying 'run rooms', what are you talking about?" I ask.

"Figures rat-man didn't tell you anything. Look at the walls. See the discs?" Grrblin asks.

Evie and I look. Three walls have a glass disc the size of a super-frisbee in the center.

"Is that one crying?" Evie asks. Each disc has a face. "And that one is screaming?"

"We call them The Fates," Grrblin says. "They're portals into the rooms. Rooms like video game dungeons. Some full of monsters. Others puzzles. Most have treasure or special items—"

"And the best ones have key mobs," I say. They're the ones to beat. That's how I'll win.

"You got it. But boss mobs are rare."

"And the door with all the locks?" Evie asks.

The fourth wall has three doors. On the left a black door. The right door is white. In the center is a golden door with seven locks. I turn and check for the shimmering door. It's gone.

"Sup," a new voice says.

"Sup sup," Grrblin says.

"These our eyes?"

I spin around and watch Grrblin fist-bump a huge kid. He's basically a smaller version of the Hulk minus the green. He's square with muscles everywhere.

Evie skips over and speaks first. "Hi! Are you Stump? You're Stump. Did you just call us eyes? Why did you call us eyes? I'm Evie, that's Charlie," she says.

"Whoa. I like her," Stump says, a big grin on his face.

Grrblin rolls his eyes then jabs a finger at my goggles. "Those eyes. Wizard Eyes. You tell us what you see."

"What I see?" I ask.

"Neither of you know how to turn them on, do you?"

"Don't even know," repeats Stump, popping a green nugget in his mouth.

Grrblin notices. "Gross, dude." He waves Evie and I over close. "Put your finger on top of the right lens. Feel the tiny bump?" I nod. "Press it and slide to the left toward your nose. You'll feel it click."

It slides easily. The Wizard Eyes click and change.

"Whoa," Evie says.

"Now look at the tables. What do you see?"

# MAGGOT BURGER

There's something freakish about all the food. It's glowing. I wander over to the closest table and pick up a burger. It's got a bluish tint.

"What do you see?" Grrblin says, peering at the burger like he's not sure what it is.

"Ya, what does it give you?" Stump asks.

I'm not sure what to do, so I close my eyes and sniff like I saw the girl do with the apple. It smells moldy and I feel it crawling around my fingers. When I open my eyes, there are maggots and roaches slithering down my arm.

"AHH!" I yell, dropping the burger.

"What? What is it?" Grrblin says, inspecting the burger but not touching it.

"It's covered in maggots!"

"Dude, chill. Inspect it. What does it say?" Grrblin motions to the side of the burger. "What does it say, like, around the burger?"

I look closer. I hate roaches. But I see words. "It says creeping death."

"Ah, that spell sucks," Stump says. "Evie, lets find tacos. Tacos always have good stuff."

"Mmm," Evie says, skipping after Stump in search of tacos.

Grrblin picks up the burger and inspects it. "Look here, Eyeball. This is magic." He holds out the burger. "I mean, that's how we get magic to play the game. That's what you do. You see, we eat, we head into a room."

He leans back, cracks his jaw, tosses the burger in and swallows it whole. Then burps so hard his whole body shakes. Clicking the button on his pack, a baseball-sized thing rushes down to his hand. Black skeleton fingers crawl around the ball.

WHOOOSH!

Grrblin flings the ball, and it explodes against the

wall, leaving a big black spot crawling with maggots and roaches scavenging what they find.

"What is that thing you threw? The baseball thing from your pack?" I ask.

"Sticky bomb. Fill 'em with magic and throw. That one had creeping death. Normally, I use magic to slow stuff down. Come here," Grrblin says, walking towards the veggie table. He snags a bunch of nasty green stuff. "Look at these. What do they say?"

I look with the Wizard Eyes, and there's a mix of words floating around the leafy vegetables.

"Snare or Root," I say. Grrblin nods, chewing a leaf while gathering more.

"What powers do you want, Eyeball?" Grrblin asks. "You get two per room run. I'm taking Snare and Root. Stump will take Bash and Poison Resist."

I knew I'd get magic powers, but I didn't know this was how I'd pick. What do I want? What should I pick?

FREE AUDIOBOOK!
JOIN THE INSIDER'S CLUB
*FREE FOR CURRENT MEMBERS TOO

CONNORGRAYSON.COM

# BLENDER
# NINJA

"Uh, I'm taking Shielding home slice," Stump says, strolling up with an armload of tacos.

I catch Evie's eye as she walks up with her own armload of items. "What powers are you getting?" I ask.

"These hairy fruits give me healing power. Not the strongest, but it sounds fast. And this," she says, lifting a jar of what looks like bubbles. "Lets me move things with my mind. How cool is that!"

"Uh, no. You're taking Poison Resist. Trust me. I have a feeling." Grrblin steals the Shielding tacos from Stump and tosses them back on the table. "So, Eyeball, what do you want? If Evie's got heals, we need some damage. How about Fireballs? Lightning bolts?"

Thinking about the games I've played, this group has a tank in Stump. He'll take damage and keep the mobs away from the rest of us. Grrblin is utility. He'll be able to lock down anything that gets loose with his snares and roots. Limiting movement of the monsters. It sounds like Evie will play healer, with a bit of utility or damage with her mind powers.

"Grrblin, what kind of damage do you do if you're taking Snare and Root?" I ask.

"Good question. Maybe you're not dead weight," he says, brandishing a small short bow from his pack. "This is one of the magical items I got in a room. Each run we make, I get a thousand arrows to use, before it's empty."

I need to do damage then. But why does he want Stump to have Poison Resist?

"Why Poison Resist?" I ask.

"Because snakes. We're due for snakes."

AH-OOH-GA! AH-OOH-GA! AH-OOH-GA!

"Beware the klaxon!" A kid sprints past, both his hands cupping his mouth, yelling.

"Beware the klaxon! Beware the klaxon!"

AH-OOH-GA! AH-OOH-GA! AH-OOH-GA!

I slap my hands to my ears and yell, "What's happening?"

"Times up. We've got to move. The Fates are waking up," Grrblin says. He takes off running towards the end of the sweets table. Stump and Evie race after him. I race after them. I notice the goblin grabbing things off tables as we go.

AH-OOH-GA! AH-OOH-GA! AH-OOH-GA!

He skids to a stop at the table with all the blenders and slams four big cups down. Then he crams a blender with his ingredients. Stump does the same thing with his own blender, adding a handful of something from Grrblin.

"What do I do?" Evie asks, glancing towards Stump.

"Throw in your goodies, then pour in that until it's about to overflow," Stump says, pointing to a jug of glowing goop in the center of the table.

"Eyeball!" Grrblin shouts. "Hurry up, get over here. Mix this up. Throw them in and blend them up. Sixty-seven seconds. Six-seven. Be precise!"

He tosses me rotten, black apples and a bunch of tiny, slimy fish with three eyes. Yuck. Mutant sardines. I try to see what powers I'll get, but I can't make it out. I don't know.

"Why is he calling you Eyeball?" Evie whispers, as we're filling our blenders with ingredients.

Probably sounding weird from plugging my nose, I

49

say, "I have no idea, but whatever." These mutant fish are the worst.

AH-OOH-GA! AH-OOH-GA! AH-OOH-GA!

"Hurry, hurry," Grrblin says. I hear his blender scream to life.

I dump my ingredients in and top them off with glowing goop from the jug on the table. I flip the switch on, squeeze my eyes shut so I can focus, and count in my head.

Forty-seven. Forty-eight.

"Beware the klaxon!"

Fifty-one, fifty-two.

"Come on, come on. We're not going to make it, dudes," Stump says.

Breathe. I hear the others turning their blenders off and pouring smoothies into cups. Opening my eyes, I see them chugging.

Sixty-three. My finger is on the switch. Sixty-six, sixty-seven.

I flip the switch off! Then I rip the blender open and pour the blend into a big red cup. Evie finishes hers, and I gawk as she glows blue and the air vibrates around her.

"Drink it on the way," Grrblin says, sprinting away. Stump takes off. Evie and I race after them.

The smell of this smoothie is the worst. Imagine combining rotten apples and sardines with bad breath. I just threw up in my mouth a little.

"Drink, home slice. Pretend it's Dr. Pepper," Stump says.

I gulp, expecting fish guts and get Dr. Pepper. Haha. Great. One more gulp and it's gone. My insides feel warm and fuzzy. I flex my fingers like a monster claw. Then I squeeze them into a fist so hard my knuckles turn white. My hand burns. I fling my fingers wide and a fireball appears, hovering over my hand.

"Ha! This is awesome!"

We skid to a stop in front of one of the glass discs. The screaming face portal. It glows and pulses with energy.

AH-OOH-GA! AH-OOH-GA! AH-OOH-GA!

The face doesn't move, but its eyes do. They cast a circle of light on the floor.

"Everybody get in the circle," Grrblin says, reaching out towards the disc. "We only get one chance to get this right. Be smart. If we die, the next group goes."

"What will be inside?" Evie asks.

"Snakes. Lots of snakes." The goblin presses The Fate's face down like a button.

The floor crumbles under us and we plummet into the pit.

# THE JELLY

 **MAGIC ATTACK** | **MELEE ATTACK**

## SEEP

THE JELLY IS A CHICKEN!
IF YOU EVER TRY TO ATTACK
ONE, DON'T LET THEM SEEP
ON YOU! THEY'LL MELT INTO
THE GROUND AND DISAPPEAR.
IF THEY'RE ANGRY YOU NEVER
KNOW WHERE THEY'LL POP UP
AND MELEE ATTACK YOU!

## SLATHER

THE JELLY WILL SNEAK UP
FROM OUT OF THE GROUND
AND SLIME YOU! GREEN, BLUE
OR RED GOOP WILL COVER
WHEREEVER THEY SLAP YOU
WITH THEIR TINY ARMS. IF
YOU'RE TOO SLOW TO GET IT
OFF, YOU MIGHT MELT A LITTLE!

## STICKY BOMBS

I slam into a cold, dirt floor. It's dark, and I can barely see.

Grrblin says, "Move slow and quiet. I can't see, but there should be a wall. Get to the wall." I only feel the goblin moving next to me. Where are Evie and Stump? I reach my hand out and feel a smooth stone wall. I scoot until my backpack hits stone, then press into the wall inching myself up.

"Hey, Eyeball, come here. Slow, slide against the wall."

I slide towards his voice, the wall's slimy and slick, until I bump into him. I have no idea where Stump and Evie are. "I can't see anything," I say.

Grrblin grabs my hand and guides it to a spot on the Wizard Eyes. He taps two times to turn them back on. "Sleep mode, just like your computer. It's annoying. That should turn on night mode," he says.

In the center of the room, coiled up inside a monster-sized glass aquarium, is an enormous snake. Hovering above the snake is a ghost wearing an old-fashioned dress with lace on the neck and sleeves. She scowls at me as she adjusts pointy glasses. Slowly, floating from side to side, she leaves a purple trail of mist behind her.

I tell Grrblin.

"Does she have a name above her head?"

I check and she does. The letters keep disappearing as she moves, but finally I make them out.

"The Angry Librarian," I say.

"Make a fireball," Grrblin says. I crinkle my forehead and squeeze my hand tight like I'm crushing something. Then I fling my fingers and open my palm flat. A fireball hovers there. It crackles quietly like wood fires do.

I glance around and notice the room is brighter. Grrblin comes close with one of his sticky bombs.

Writing weeds and vines crawl up his arm and away from the fireball. He holds the sticky bomb above the fireball.

"Push it in. We've got to combine them."

I shove my hand until the fireball hits the bottom of the sticky bomb. The weeds catch fire and smell bitter like my hands after I pick a dandelion weed. It resists, but I keep pushing until the fire goes inside the sticky bomb. Grrblin chucks it towards the ceiling in the middle of the room.

It explodes right above The Angry Librarian. Weeds and burning vines scatter, covering the ceiling. The room lights on fire. The snake's massive head creaks as he lifts it up towards the ceiling. A two-foot-long tongue licks the air.

The Angry Librarian hesitates then swings towards Grrblin and me. Her glare makes me feel frozen inside and like I weigh a million pounds. Motion to one side draws her attention, and I follow her gaze. Stump and Evie are crawling along a wall towards us. They freeze.

The Angry Librarian stares back at me, and I see her ghost jaws open, revealing a set of fangs. She flies towards me.

"AHH!" I yell, slamming against the wall.

The ghost stops and laughs. She flies in circles around the room, kicking up dust so it becomes hard to see her.

Then she screams.

I plug my ears with my fingers, but it doesn't help. The scream shakes me down to my guts. I hear glass shatter.

I watch The Angry Librarian fly upwards. Pausing below the ceiling, her head snaps back, and glowing blue eyes drill into me. She smiles, and a black tongue snakes across her fangs before she glides through the ceiling.

"That's a key mob for sure," Grrblin says, hopping up and down. "Where's the others? We need a plan."

# SNAKE
# FLIPPING

Stump and Evie sneak up, hugging the wall. Evie is pale and breathing heavy.

"Did you see that ghost?" Evie asks, trying to catch her breath. "It stared at me so long I felt frozen, and black butterflies fluttered in my belly. It was the worst!"

"It's a key mob. It has to be. Eyeball said it's The Angry Librarian," Grrblin says.

HISS!

Stump slowly moves in front of us.

The dust settles, and I peer across the room looking for the snake in the glass aquarium.

"I heard glass shatter when the ghost screamed, does that mean..." Evie asks, standing next to me and scanning the center of the room.

"It means the snake's cage shattered, and it's out. A key mob guardian won't be easy," Grrblin says, summoning a sticky bomb to each hand. He chucks them into the center of the room. They burst open and bury the dirt floor in weeds and vines. "That should slow it down."

I see the snake just outside the shattered aquarium. It uncoils as its head snaps forward. Slithering towards us, I hear it snap through the weeds and vines. Stopping, it stares and flicks its tongue in the air. I feel like it's trying to figure out which of us to eat first. Grrblin picks out another sticky bomb and holds it ready to throw.

"Stump. Stump, you ready?"

Stump grunts and drops into a stance. Like the one they teach you in sports or martial arts. Feet wide and stable. One foot back, one foot forward. He raises his right arm in front of him like a shield.

Grrblin and I move behind Stump. Evie skips to the right.

I don't know.

"Evie!"

"Let me try something," she says, lightly touching a hand to her temple. The other hand she aims at the snake.

Blue sparkles flash across the enormous snake. It watches Evie and snaps its jaws at her. Fire drips from the ceiling into a pool of water. I hear it fizzle as it hits and goes out.

"There's water behind the snake," I say.

"Fireball. Get a fireball," Grrblin says, without taking his eyes off the enormous snake. "This could be bad."

Evie makes a scooping motion with her hand like she's pitching a softball. "HI-YA!" she yells.

The snake flips into the air. Its head cracks into the ceiling and chunks of stone rain onto the dirt floor. The snake falls back down, and the room rumbles from its weight.

HISS! HISS!

The snake slithers at top speed. Away from us!

"Stop it!" Grrblin launches a sticky bomb, and it explodes behind the snake in a mess of green. Stump sprints after the snake, and I stand there.

"Uhh." I have no idea what to do. I toss a fireball and it misses by about fifty feet. Why did I stop playing baseball?

The snake dives through the air, splashing down into water. We watch his whole body slide down a hole and disappear. I swear the thing is twenty feet long.

"Do we chase it?" I ask.

"Naw. It'll be back," Grrblin says, motioning for me to make another sticky fireball with him.

I scan the room. It's empty and eerily quiet. Grrblin and I finish, and he chucks the sticky fireball at the ceiling so we don't run out of light.

"Yo, Evie. Nice one. That's a huge hole," Stump says, staring through the super-sized hole in the ceiling.

"Did you notice the color of that snake, Stump?" Grrblin asks.

"Gray," he says. "Pretty sure. Little speckles too, like last time."

"Want another basher arm?"

"Definitely," Stump says.

# KITE
# THEM

It's not long before the water bubbles like it's boiling. It even spills out of the pool and spreads across the room.

"It's coming back. Get behind," Stump says, stepping up towards the water. "Evie, stay close. I'll need heals, but let the snake get to me. Don't toss it, okay?"

"Roger. Ten four," Evie says, adjusting her pool floaties.

Grrblin tosses a bunch of sticky bombs around the

water and lets the green mess take over. He shrugs, backs up, and whips out his bow.

I move to the other side of Stump, staying behind him, but not so much I can't see the water. I close my eyes and make two fists. I squeeze hard enough to make my knuckles crack. I fling my fingers open. I might not be Jack Sullivan, but I've got fireballs. Boom boom.

BADABOOM!

The water explodes, splashing the ceiling. The firelight sizzles, half of it dying. When the water hits the floor, I realize it's mostly not water. It's moving. Slithering. Dozens of normal-sized snakes stand up.

HISS! HISS! HISSSSS! HISSSSSSS!

"Run run run!" Stump yells, scooping up Evie piggyback style.

"Ohcrapohcrapohcrap," Grrblin says, taking off past me.

"AHH!" I sprint to catch up.

We reach a corner, and Grrblin pauses. "Kite them, we've got to kite them."

"We don't have a kite, what are you—" I say, looking at Grrblin like he's cuckoo.

"Get them to chase us, and we run them around." He spins his finger in circles to explain. It doesn't help. "It'll work. Stump! We'll kite, you pick them off."

Grrblin covers the floor in sticky bombs, vines and weeds. Enough to slow anything down. He pops off arrow after arrow at the snakes. He yells at me to launch fireballs.

I throw heaters. Hey, I'm allowed to pretend I know baseball things.

The snakes take enough damage they get angry and speed-slither towards us.

"Keep hitting them and moving around so they can't get to you," Grrblin says, firing another handful of arrows. "Stump will get them."

I glance at Stump, and he's got about five snakes in front of him snapping at his arm. Evie is nearby, and she's HI-YA attacking two snakes which got past him.

I'm not sure how he's going to "get them" like Grrblin said. Two snakes snap, and Stump swings his arm up. Both snakes bite into him. He stumbles. Three more snakes dart at him, and I watch snake fangs sink into his flesh. Stump drops to his knees.

"Noo!" I yell, lunging towards them to help.

"Eyeball! Stop, they're good. Evie's got him," Grrblin says. I skid to a stop and observe. Evie is doing something that makes Stump glow. "Those are rock snakes. He's catching them on purpose. He's got Poison Resist."

Ten snakes are clamped on Stump's arm. They hang there, not moving, like a rock. Rock snakes. I squint. Stump's arm is gray up to his elbow and, well, bigger. Wider. Like a small tree trunk.

Stump slams his stone-arm into the ground, and all

the frozen snakes snap in half or shatter. Rock explodes everywhere. When Stump pulls his stone-fist out of the ground, there's a big hole. Wow. Awesome. Basher arm.

Grrblin and I still have dozens of snakes snapping at our heels. I keep running in circles, chucking fireballs, and he keeps shooting arrows.

Stump runs up and bashes a big group of snakes off to one side, and they shatter. Evie flings a pair of snakes into the ceiling, and they burst apart.

It doesn't take long before all the snakes are little pieces of rock spread across the dirt floor.

"No loot and no door to the next room. What gives?" Stump asks.

# THE SNAKE BOSS

 **MAGIC ATTACK**   **MELEE ATTACK**

## SPAWN

WHEN IT GETS IN TROUBLE, IT WILL RUN AWAY AND EXPLODE INTO A TON OF SMALLER SNAKES! STOP IT BEFORE IT CAN GET AWAY OR YOU JUST MIGHT GET OVERRUN BY A BILLION LITTLE ROCK SNAKES!

## SQUEEZE

THE SNAKE BOSS WANTS TO WRAP YOU UP IN A BIG HUG. A VERY DEADLY HUG! IF IT CAN GET CLOSE TO YOU IT WILL WRAP ITS BODY AROUND AND AROUND YOU, UNTIL YOU FALL ASLEEP, AND THEN IT WILL SQUEEZE YOU UNTIL YOU POP!

KNOCK
KNOCK

The room is empty. No snakes. No loot. No door. No boss.

"What's the deal," I say. "Shouldn't something be happening?" If this is basically a video game, then something should be happening. We just cleared the first stage. We should get treasure, a door to another room, or a boss with fantastic loot.

But nothing.

"Check the walls," Grrblin says, walking back towards the entrance. "I bet there's a hidden door somewhere. Feel around in the cracks."

Opposite the goblin, I search the walls for cracks. When I find one, I dig my fingernails in and pull, hoping it's a hidden door. Even though our custom-made fireball vine-lights are near death the room is brighter. I figure it's the size of a small playground.

Evie hops onto the stones and stares at the hole in the ceiling. "Can we go that way?"

"That's like fifty feet up," I say.

"I can hi-ya you up there. Find a rope or something and you can pull me up."

"And if I screw up and crack my head like the snake? Ouch. Game over," I say, summoning a fireball and flipping it into a random wall. It dies quickly in the dirt-slime of the wall.

Stump drags his stone-arm through the dirt as he circles the room, checking for cracks and secret doors.

"What if I just bash a hole in the wall?" Stump asks.

"Don't be dumb, that'd be—" Grrblin says.

BOOM!

BOOM! BOOM!

Stump slams his stone-fist into one wall. Then another. Each time he slams a wall, dirt rains down and dust poofs into the air.

BOOM! BOOM! BOOM!

"Dude, give it a break!"

Stump plops down in the middle of the room and leans against the stones. "This sucks," he says, slamming his stone-fist into the ground.

THUD!

"What was that?" I ask, darting over.

Water seeps out of the ground where Stump hit it. It reminds me of a leaky hose slowly making a mud puddle. I stick my fingers into the mud spot and wiggle them around. The ground gives, and more water leaks out onto the dirt. It feels rough, but it's smooth like wood.

"Hit it again," I say, pointing to the mud spot. It's now about the size of a fist. Stump bashes it again. Something cracks. "Evie, get down here. Would you move these stones?"

Stump and I scurry back. Evie jumps off the stones and does her blue sparkle dance. The stones skid across the room and crash into the far wall.

"What's going on?" Grrblin asks from behind me. I turn and see him studying the mud spot. "We need to look for the door or we're stuck in this room."

"No, this is it. This is the door. I know it," I say. "Hit it again."

Stump hurls his stone-fist down.

BOOM!

"Harder. Really hard!"

CRACK!

The door shatters, wood splinters shoot out of the ground, and mud flies. Flinching, I twist away. Hearing a whooshing sound, I peek back over my shoulder. Water rushes into the room, creating a muddy mess. I wallow into the center, reach my hand down, and break away pieces of the destroyed wooden door to make a hole. Once it's the size of a sewer drain, I stop and peer down through a water tunnel.

"There's a room down there. Check it out. Help me break the rest of this wood," I say to Evie. Her eyes are wide, and she's backpedaling to the edge of the seeping water.

"How deep is it?" she asks, adjusting her pool floaties.

I peer down the water tunnel. "I don't know. Maybe three swimming pools. Will you help me?" I ask, staring at her so hard I crinkle my forehead.

"I want to, but..."

Grrblin and Stump crowd near the mud hole. "Yup, another room," Stump says.

"Nice work, Eyeball," Grrblin says. "Now swim down and open the real door."

"What are you talking about?"

"Swim down. There's got to be a button or switch down there. It triggers a door up here. You go down, trigger it, and we'll meet you then go find the boss."

"You're nuts. I'm not swimming down there." I peer

down the tunnel. It's medium-far for sure. "I can't hold my breath that long."

"What's your point?"

"Ya, swim down, dude," Stump says.

"My point? Uh... I need to breathe." I side-step away from the tunnel entrance and Grrblin grabs my shoulder.

"Hey. Don't," I say, as he shoves me towards the water.

"You're good. Swim down, Eyeball. Remember the mutant fish you ate?" Grrblin grabs my backpack and yanks me closer to the water.

"I'm not going down there! You're crazy!" I try to scramble past Grrblin and water splashes onto Evie.

"Hey. Careful," Stump says. Evie freezes and looks like she's seen another ghost.

Grrblin shoves me hard. I trip over a stone piece and plunge into the water tunnel. It's warm, and there're bubbles around my legs as I kick to stay afloat. It tastes salty like ocean water.

Grrblin turns to Stump. "Push him under, don't let him up. He'll swim down once he figures it out."

# THE FRIDGE

Stump's hand grips the top of my head before he forces me down.

"Hey okay okay this is crazy. Stump stop. Dude no," I shout, grasping and slapping his hand. His grip is as solid as his stone-arm.

He shoves me under the water. I squeeze my eyes closed.

GASP! AWK! GAK!

Sucking water in, I choke right away. I cough, trying to keep water out of my mouth. I hold my breath. My body shakes and squirms. I can't help it, I feel like I'm someone's puppet.

I can't get away from Stump's hand on my head.

My chest burns. My lungs ache.

AHH! I need to breathe!

I can't hold it anymore. I breathe, expecting to choke.

And start giggling. I giggle so hard my belly aches. I breathe in deep until I'm about to pop. It feels weird, but it's awesome. I can breathe. I glance up through the water and catch Stump's eye. I wave a thumbs up.

His face relaxes. He smiles and releases my head.

Those tiny, slimy, three-eyed fish... I love them. They granted me the power to breathe underwater. Forever Breath. I'll call it Forever Breath.

I scream that I'll be right back. Stump and Grrblin can't hear me. I figure they'll wait. Maybe figure out what's up with Evie. She was acting strange.

I kick and flip around towards the room below. It's far, but I'm a good swimmer. Using my arms, I rip through the water and realize it's hard to swim with a backpack. I cinch the straps tighter. The farther I go, the clearer it gets.

The room appears familiar. The floor must be dirt, and I think I can make out slither marks. What am I going to do when I reach the bottom? I'll break through the barrier, drop from the ceiling, and hope. Hope I don't break my face nose-diving fifty feet. And hope the place isn't crawling with snakes.

I'm in trouble. What happens in this game when you die?

I hover and float at the end of the water tunnel. Here goes. My hand slices through the barrier, and I plunge into the room and slam into the dirt floor. Oof.

Before moving, I peek around. In front of me are snake statues. They make me think of mutant-cobras. It's the extra eye.

No sign of other snakes, but I hear a buzzing sound. I stand and turn towards the noise.

It's a refrigerator.

## LOTS OF S'S

A refrigerator?

I step over to the fridge first. Please, you would too. Why is a fridge in the middle of a video game dungeon? I pull the handle, and it's stuck. Yanking hard, the entire thing shakes but won't open. Not stuck. Locked.

This is what the teacher's lounge is like. There are snacks and sodas in the fridge, cold and crisp. But I'm locked out. Forbidden. Ugh.

I peek behind the fridge, searching for a door. Maybe this is like the wardrobe from that one book. If I can get the fridge open, there will be a staircase up to the first room. The only things behind the fridge are cobwebs and slimy, slick dirt walls.

Scanning the room, I see a hatch-door in the corner opposite the fridge. Way up by the ceiling. There's a small ledge running along the wall from the hatch. It curves around and ends above the fridge like an unfinished train track. On top of the fridge is a gigantic bowl. I jump and try to see what's in the bowl, but it's too high.

Dragging my hand along the wall, I work my way to the snake statues across the room. Maybe there'll be a crack or outline of a secret door.

Nothing.

Squatting in front of the statues, without touching them, I inspect them for a button or switch.

The statues are identical. They're mutant-cobras about two feet tall with three eyes. Two eyes are where you'd expect, they're shifty and glow red as they follow me.

Their mouths fixed in a snarl, revealing fangs sharp as knives. Between the fangs is the third eye, a polished snake-eye stone the size of a gobstopper.

I lean in and check out the stone. There's a light

hissing sound. Twisting, I get my ear closer. Is the hissing coming from the statue? I lick my fingers and gently hold them up to the snake's jaw. My fingers go icy as air leaks between the fangs. There must be a hole behind the stone.

Hmm.

With a finger, I press the snake-eye stone between the fangs. It moves. Dropping to my knees, I curl my head around to peek inside the mutant-cobra's mouth. There's a track cut at the top of the snake's mouth and a small hole at the back of the throat. I press the stone again and it grinds down the track.

What happens if I force the stone back and cover the hole leaking air? I don't know. I must slide my hand inside the mutant-cobra's mouth to do it. I rub the back of my neck.

This could be bad.

I reach out, slowly, with my hand and pause in front of the first statue's mouth.

What will happen when I press this? The room floods? I trigger a trapdoor and a million snakes slither out, hungry and itching to eat? My heart booms in my ears.

My hand is too big to get past the fangs all at once. I slide in two fingers and press the snake-eye stone back, then twist my hand to slide past the fangs. The stone moves easily, and clicks into the hole at the back of the snake's throat.

Jerking my hand out of the mutant-cobra's mouth, I leap away from the statue. Scanning the room, I search for changes.

Nothing. I don't know.

I kneel, slide my hand in the second statue's mouth, and press the snake-eye stone again. Click.

On my right and left the walls inch towards each other. Making the room smaller. Not good.

The hissing air is stronger in the third statue. Sweat drips down my back as I strain to click the snake-eye stone into the hole.

Near the ceiling, the hatch-door clanks open. An old, rusty cannonball barrels through, and runs down the ledge towards the refrigerator. About halfway it cracks into an invisible barrier and stops. Grr.

The next statue must unlock the gate so the cannonball can pass. Slipping my hand into the last statue's mouth, I slam the stone down its throat.

PSHHHH!

Dust fires out of the wall and blasts me in the face. A panel pops open to reveal another snake statue. Twice the size of the others, the snake-eye stone is enormous. I rub my eyes to clear the dust. It reminds me of an everlasting gobstopper. I stand up, grip the stone in my hand, and start pressing.

The snake's mouth slowly creaks shut.

I yank my arm back, and the mouth stops closing. I glance around the room. Nothing. Wait! The bottom barrier of the water tunnel is glowing, water drips onto the floor like a leaky faucet.

I must put my entire arm in the mutant-cobra's mouth to get the stone to the back of its throat. My hands sweat. I squeeze the snake-eye stone, hard. Sweat drips into my eyes and stings. I blink fast to get it out and jam the stone down the snake's throat.

The snake's mouth snaps shut on my arm!

"AHH!" I scream, trying to pull my arm out.

Yanking, wrenching, and prying at the snake's mouth with my free hand, I'm stuck! It feels like my arm is in a Chinese finger trap. The harder I try, the tighter it gets.

CLUNK!

I whip towards the sound and see the cannonball barrel down the ledge again. It gains speed, rounding the corner.

I hear the footsteps of more rain. The water tunnel! The barrier is collapsing. Water pours into the room. Faster and faster by the second.

The cannonball plunges into the bowl on top of the fridge. I hear another click-clunk, and the fridge pops open. Perfect. *Now* it's open. I roll my eyes.

Water and mud splash everywhere. The barrier gone,

water gushes into the room like a waterfall. I snap my eyes shut and feel mud splatter my face.

"Hey, Eyeball!" Grrblin shouts from the first room. "You alive down there?"

"I'm stuck! I'm stuck in a stinking snake statue!"

"Cannonball!"

# THE ANGRY LIBRARIAN

## MAGIC ATTACK
### SCREAM

THE ANGRY LIBRARIAN HAS NO PATIENCE FOR MAGIC. USE IT IN HER PRESENCE AND SHE'LL LET LOOSE A SCREAM THAT'LL RATTLE YOUR BONES. WHILE YOU COWER IN FEAR, ANY MAGIC YOU HAD IS SNATCHED AWAY. GONE FOREVER!

## MELEE ATTACK
### HURL

MAKE A MOVE TOWARDS THE ANGRY LIBRARIAN AND YOU'RE ON HER HIT LIST. SHE'LL SWOOP IN AND STEAL YOU UP IN A CLAWED HAND! SAY YOUR GOODBYES BECAUSE YOU'RE ABOUT TO BE HURLED DOWN A DEEP, DARK HOLE!

# CHERRY COKE

SPLASH!

Grrblin lands the biggest cannonball ever. He's nuts. I swam down that tunnel. It's long. I don't know if I'd be able to jump.

"Big man, come on, stop being a chicken. Jump!" Grrblin yells up the tunnel.

This cannonball will be epic.

"Yooooo," Stump yells. His voice echoes off the walls and vibrates the room.

SMACK!

I cringe for him. Biggest belly-flop ever. That left a mark. Stump groans as he pulls himself up, glances around, and rubs his stomach.

"Evie! Ready?" Stump yells, peering through the hole in the ceiling. "Don't worry, I'll catch you."

Blue sparkles float into the room, and not long after, Evie. She floats into Stump's arms like the good witch from Oz. She might as well be riding a bubble.

"Thanks," she says, scanning the room. "Can you put me on top of the fridge?"

I don't know.

"You need to tell him," Grrblin says. "It might be important."

Evie glances my way and quickly averts her gaze. She motions for the goblin to go ahead.

"Water and Evie don't mix. She's scared."

"It's not a big deal," Stump says, lifting Evie to the top of the fridge.

That's why she was acting strange in the other room. The pool floaties! "I'm scared of lots of things. It's good. Thanks for telling me," I say.

"You stuck?" Stump asks, wading through the water towards me.

"Pretty much." I see Grrblin bolt towards the fridge.

"It was locked and wouldn't open until this mutant-cobra trapped me over here."

The goblin yanks the door open wide. "Not anymore," he says. "Can't believe we got a fridge. I haven't had a fridge spawn in forever."

Stump freezes and spins around. "Fridge?"

Bottles clink together as Grrblin shuffles around in the fridge. There are sounds of drawers opening and closing. What's he looking for?

"What's the big deal about a fridge?" I ask.

"A fridge means power-ups. Which means boss loot soon. Fantastic boss loot. Last time, I got my bow."

Stump shoves his head inside the fridge beside Grrblin, and they both rummage around. They're talking, but I can't make anything out. They hand Evie a bunch of blue bottles. Grrblin slips orange and yellow bottles into his leather pack.

"Hey, a little help?" I say, thinking about what the rat-man said. I'd be in big trouble if I was alone.

Stump turns, and a huge grin crosses his face. He pops open a bottle with red liquid and chugs it as he lunges through the water towards me.

"Uh," I say. "I'm sure you just grew a bunch taller."

"Eyeball, close your eyes, quick," Grrblin says.

Stump raises his stone-arm. "No, no, no, wait," I say. He rips his basher arm through the air, I cringe, snap my eyes closed, and wait for the impact.

CRACK!

The snake's mouth blasts apart, and I rip my arm out. Wiping sweat from my face, I glance at Stump and nod.

"No problemo," Stump says, chugging something green now.

The everlasting gobstopper is in the pile of rubble. I pick it up and slip it in my pocket.

"Eyeball, come here. Drink this." Grrblin holds up a glass bottle full of black liquid.

"What is it?" I ask, shaking the bottle. The liquid clings to the sides like syrup.

Grrblin downs a yellow bottle. "It's magic. A power boost or rare quest. You never know until you do." He pops the top on an orange bottle and starts drinking. "I love this one, reminds me of orange popsicles."

"Mine tastes like blue raspberry," Evie says.

I turn on the Wizard Eyes and inspect the black syrup. "Why do I have to drink the black one?"

"Only color left," Stump says, then burps. He's leaning against the wall near the busted mutant-cobra statue. Empty bottles float in the surrounding water. I'm pretty sure he's napping.

"He's right," Grrblin says. "Stump is always red and green. I have orange and yellow. Evie's color is blue, because sparkles. We've tried other colors before, and they do nothing for us. Only ones left in the fridge are the black ones. Never seen them, actually. Fun stuff. Drink up, Eyeball."

The Wizard Eyes tell me the black syrup grants Heart of Darkness. Fantastic. Sounds amazing.

I don't know.

"What do yours do?" I ask.

"Yellow makes me fast. Well, faster. Orange gives me higher accuracy when I use my bow."

"Red makes big. Green makes strong. Me Hulk," Stump says, chuckling to himself.

I glance at Evie, and she shrugs. She's not sitting on the fridge but floating above it. Wisps of blue mist surround her.

I pop the top of my bottle and sniff. It smells like sour blackberries. When I dip the tip of my tongue in I'm reminded of cherry coke. Totally not my favorite. At least it's not licorice. I pour the syrup in my mouth and swish it around, thinking.

Do I really want to swallow this? I have no idea what it will do? It might do nothing. Hopefully, it won't turn me into a little goblin monster like Grrblin or a Hulk like Stump. My mom told me this story once, where a guy wakes up as a cockroach. I don't know. She's kinda weird.

My mouth is on fire. It's like the worst mouthwash ever. The more I swish, the worse it gets. A monster's mouthwash. Swallowing, it goes down cool.

"Ugh, it burns," I say.

"Swallow faster or don't," Stump says.

"Some people say the longer you can keep it in your mouth, the more powerful the effect," Grrblin says. "Two kids burned their mouth off."

Gross.

"Feel anything?" Stump asks, cracking an eye and peeking at me.

Closing my eyes, I pay attention to my body. Everything tingles a little. There's something happening in my chest. Warm and slow, like when you drink hot chocolate. I shrug.

"It's not always fast-acting," Grrblin says, handing me three more bottles. I slip them into my backpack.

Cold, frozen fingers wrap around my heart and squeeze. My stomach flips. What was that?

"Time to go. Stump, get up, you've got to move the fridge," Grrblin says.

# GHOST
# WALLS

Stump leans a shoulder into the fridge and pushes like a bulldozer.

SCREEEEEEEEECH!

It's like fingernails on a chalkboard. I slap my hands over my ears and cringe so hard my insides feel twisted.

Grrblin inspects the spot where the fridge used to be. He dunks his hand in the water and feels around. "Got it," he says, yanking a hatch on the floor open.

The water in the room rushes down the hole. Of course! Why didn't I look under the fridge?

I don't know.

Grrblin kneels down and sticks his head through the hatch. Ten seconds later he pops back up.

"Pretty dark. Eyeball fireball," Grrblin says. I summon a fireball and combine it with one of his sticky bombs.

Grrblin tosses it down the hatch, and it shatter-pops like a light bulb exploding. The goblin jumps down. Stump follows.

Evie hops down from the fridge, and we peer into the darkness together. Orange-red light flickers where the fiery weed-vines smolder, and I see shadows of our group moving to the right.

"I have a bad feeling about this," Evie says, jumping down the hatch. Blue sparkles fly up from her feet as she hits the ground. She's getting good with that power.

Flipping to my belly, I slide my feet down as far as I can until I'm hanging from my hands. Letting go, I drop a few feet and land in firelight.

BANG!

The hatch slams closed above us and melts into the ceiling. We couldn't go back if we wanted to.

Wonderful.

Chasing Evie down a narrow hall, I realize the farther I go, the wider it gets. Turning a corner, Grrblin, Stump, and Evie are standing at the ledge of a huge cavern. They're staring down at something.

There's a stone bridge sloping up as it crosses to the other side of the cavern. It's barely wide enough for one person.

"What is it?" I ask. There's no floor here. It just drops about a hundred feet into a gigantic pool. Swimming circles down in the pool is a snake-worm monster.

"Huge water snake," Grrblin says.

"More like wormongulous," Evie says, peeking over Stump's shoulder.

Suddenly, the monster leaps out of the water and flies at us.

RRRROOOOOOAAAARRRRRRR!

Its jaws crack open as it gets close, and millions of razor-sharp teeth line its gullet.

The monster snaps its jaws and plummets back into the pool. Water splashes the cavern walls. Grrblin and Stump stumble back, soaking wet. I search for Evie and find her huddled in a corner behind a tunnel wall. Mist hangs in the air.

"We have to cross," I say, pointing to the bridge. "Maybe there's another room up there."

With a toe, I press down on the first stone of the bridge to see if it holds. The stones appear to be floating in mid-air. As soon as I apply some pressure, it cracks.

"Eyeball," Grrblin says, sounding nervous.

Pressing harder... The stone crumbles, breaks apart under my foot, and zooms towards the water. Losing my balance, I stumble forward. Stump grabs my backpack and tugs me back.

"Two steps, it breaks," Grrblin says. "Two steps, four of us. Even if we go fast, the stone will break before— what is that?"

Whispers shout from behind me, and I spin around. The hallway behind us isn't dark, it's like a black hole. There's nothing there. Nothing I can see.

"Someone's knocking. Knocking on the walls," Evie cries from the corner.

"Stay here," I say, dragging myself into the hallway. I summon a fireball and hold it up. Its light licks the walls. I peer around the corner. "There's nothing here. It's nothing—"

A psycho wind whips through the hall, and I go stiff. My mind races, my heart rumbles. Run. I want to run.

Everything goes cold and I can't stop shivering.

A purple mist snakes around my feet and slithers up my legs. I can't move. It chokes me.

I hear *her* laugh.

"Eyeball..." Grrblin says behind me. "Freaking me out. What do you see?"

Her gray face drifts out of the black hole. It's covered

in bloody, oozing spots. There's the stench of dead things on her breath.

The Angry Librarian jolts forward and grasps my neck in a clawed hand. My feet dangle as she lifts me high off the ground.

Evie screams behind me.

Ghosts glide out of the walls and shuffle past me. They glow purple as they stagger through The Angry Librarian's mist.

I summon a fireball, and a ghost hesitates. The Angry Librarian studies me curiously. The look turns into an evil glare. She screams, and my fireball goes out.

"Run..." I choke out.

"Get behind me," I hear Stump say. "Evie. Heals. Lots of heals."

The Angry Librarian flies above her hordes of ghosts as they attack my friends. She hovers over the cavern, and I spot the water below.

"Watch. Their end." Her voice is old and sounds like gravel.

CRACK!

Stump bashes three ghosts into the wall, and they disappear in puffs of smoke. He grunts as others lash and land blows on his back. Evie reaches out for him, and he glows.

Grrblin flings sticky bombs down the hall. Weeds and vines tangle the ghosts, slowing them down. Until more glide out of the walls and rush forward. He fires arrow after arrow, each hitting the bullseye. Ghosts go up in puffs of smoke.

More ghosts glide out of the walls. More. More. More.

"There's too many!" Evie yells.

"Stump, now," Grrblin says, backing up to the edge of the ledge. "The bridge. We need to get them out."

The ghosts continue to shuffle forward. More glide out of the walls.

My friends scramble and run. Grrblin bolts across the bridge, cracking each stone. Stump carries Evie on his back as they dash across. The stones break and fall into the water as they go by.

Once they reach the other side, a shimmer door appears. Above the shimmer door is a sign.

*Library*

Grrblin walks up to the ledge and catches my eye. After unfastening the tubes from his arms, he drops his pack to the ground and rummages through it. He pulls out an orange bottle and as he guzzles the drink, a bright glow shrouds his body and bow.

The Angry Librarian swoops around and hisses at him. Grrblin raises the bow and draws back the string.

"Evie, catch him," Grrblin says.

An arrow zips right by me and thuds into The Angry

Librarian's shoulder. She shrieks, and I tumble towards the water.

The maw of the water snake snaps open and I flail my arms, hoping it'll slow me down when blue sparkles seize my body. Twisting around, there's Evie on the ledge! She makes a huge pulling motion like she's in a game of tug-o-war, and I fly right at her.

I tuck before hitting the ledge and bowl through Evie and Stump, knocking them down like bowling pins.

The Angry Librarian screams so hard it jolts my bones. She flies towards us and snatches Grrblin up in a vice grip. She spins and hurls him down the cavern. When I hear the water snake's million teeth crack down, my insides cringe.

Evie and Stump dive through the shimmer door. Grabbing Grrblin's pack and bow, I leap through too.

# SLIME
# DEATH

I slam into a cold vinyl floor. It's sticky and smells like plastic. I don't move and just close my eyes. Squeeze them tight because they feel like I'm chopping onions.

"I can't believe it," Stump says, smashing his stone-hand into the floor. "I should have had them!"

"I can't believe he's gone," Evie says, picking up Grrblin's pack.

Too scared, I didn't help my friend. "Grrblin's gone

because of me. It's my fault we lost," I say, sitting up and hugging my knees.

"What are you talking about? You took on The Angry Librarian by yourself," Evie says.

"I—I just wanted to run. I couldn't think of anything else. The scream…"

"She's a key mob," Stump says. "Key mobs suck." He wanders up to the opening in front of us and looks out.

The room we landed in is about the size of a bathroom. It's all vinyl, and there's a doorway but no door.

Hanging my head, I see everything replay. All the things I could have done. Should have done. I realize I did what Grrblin would have done. I took action. I moved forward. That's what he's always doing. He was always pushing us to keep going. And he saved me. That means something.

"What do we do now?" Evie asks.

"We take action. We win," I say, standing up and joining Stump. "Where are we?"

"Ghost library, basically."

He's right. A huge circular librarian's desk divides the room. On the far side of the desk are shelves of books. Between us and the desk are work tables scattered with ghosts. The ghosts seem to be reading and scribbling on paper. They're studying?

I don't know.

"How hard were the ghosts you guys fought when I was—"

"They're easy. Hit them once and they poof. They just don't fight fair and come in huge numbers," Stump says.

"They hit you with a lot of damage though," Evie says. "Healing was hard."

"Where do you think The Angry Librarian is?"

"She always shows up at the worst time. If we fight her ghosts, she'll show up," I say, thinking. "Evie, can I have that pack?"

Evie hands me Grrblin's pack. I swing my own off my back and kneel. I pull the items out of my backpack and put them into Grrblin's. There are the Goblin Grub ingredients. My Wizard Eyes try to tell me what powers they have, but I don't pay attention. I dig deep and pick out the big, sticky ball of green string. Finally, I move over the bottles of black syrup. I'm still not sure what they do.

"You going to wear that?" Stump asks.

"Why not? Maybe I can get it to work," I say, tightening Grrblin's pack on my back. I flip the tubes over my shoulders and buckle the straps down along my arms.

"Here." Evie hands me Grrblin's bow. I pull back the string, and an arrow magically appears. I let up slowly, and the arrow disappears. Nice. Grrblin always stored the bow in the top pocket of the pack, so I slip it in.

Popping the button on the pack, a sticky bomb shoots down the tube, and I catch it in my hand. Awesome. They're empty because I don't have Snare magic like Grrblin. Maybe I can use them for something else.

"So what's the plan?" Stump and Evie ask at the same time.

Studying the library again, there are two tables closest to us. The one to the right has three ghosts. The left table has one.

"I'll sneak up on the solo ghost there. If you're right, one fireball should take him out. Can you guys take the table to the right and those ghosts?"

"No problemo."

"Let's meet back here. We can slowly work our way through the library and take out all the ghosts. Then, when The Angry Librarian shows up, we only worry about her."

Evie and Stump slip into the library and crouch down. They creep along the wall to the right. It looks like they'll sneak behind the ghosts and fight along the wall.

I slide to the left along the wall towards the solo ghost. He's facing me, but reading a book. My plan is to sneak within fireball range.

CRACK!

Stump must be bashing.

HI-YA!

Evie must be flinging.

The ghost in front of me hears it too. His head snaps up, and he sees me. Stump and Evie attacking is super-loud. I squeeze my fingers into a fist and fling my fingers open for a fireball. Nothing happens.

I don't know.

The ghost bolts up from the table and glides towards me. I try to summon a fireball again. Please work.

Fizzle. Fail.

I'm in trouble.

The ghost hurls a ball of slime at me, and it slams into my chest. Ack! I turn and sprint towards Stump and Evie.

Another ball of slime smacks into my back. Ugh. I'm getting slower, like I'm running through the mud. This must be how it feels to take damage. I try for another fireball. What is happening? Oh no. The scream. When The Angry Librarian had me, she screamed, and my fireball went out. She stole my magic...

Stump and Evie are fighting their last ghost. There's a shriek behind me, and another ball of slime blasts me in the back of the knee. It won't bend! Dragging my leg along, I tell myself to keep moving.

"Stump! Evie!"

The ghost swings around in front of me, blocking the view of my friends. His mouth cracks open in a joker grin. He's got fangs like The Angry Librarian. He pulls back a fist and pummels me in the stomach.

Everything goes black.

# THE GHOST MINION

 **MAGIC ATTACK** | **MELEE ATTACK**

## SCREER

## HEAD BUTT

THE GHOST MINION OPENS ITS GAPING MOUTH AND LOOKS LIKE IT'LL SCREAM, BUT INSTEAD IT SCREERS! IF YOU'RE CAUGHT LOOKING AT THE TWIRLY THING IN THEIR THROAT YOU'LL SEE YOUR FUTURE...AND IT'S NOT GOOD!

THE GHOST MINION IS A CHEATER! THEY'LL SURROUND YOU ON ALL SIDES AND HEAD BUTT YOU AROUND LIKE A PINBALL! THEY SMACK HARD, SO GET AWAY QUICK. YOU WON'T SURVIVE MORE THAN A FEW HEAD BUTTS!

# ZOMBIE ARCADE

"Your business is important to us, and we appreciate your patience. You have one customer in front of you. Please wait," a woman's voice says, followed by cheesy hold music.

I don't know.

I'm in a cold, sterile room. It reminds me of a doctor's office. Or maybe the dentist's. It's so clean I'm afraid to touch anything.

I'm sitting on a couch. There's a young woman behind a desk in front of me.

She jots on a piece of paper and then calls to me. "Number twenty-two. I'll call you when it's your turn. Won't be long," she says.

To my left are two doors. One black and one white. The black door cracks open, and I see lights flashing. Wandering over, I peek inside. There's a kid playing an old arcade game, with joysticks and a hungry coin slot. It's a game called Magic Eaters. Beside him is a table covered in empty bottles. Except one, that's full of black syrup, just like those I have.

"What the..." I say out loud.

The kid turns to me and stares, and I stumble back. His eyes are hollow sockets, deep and black. On his forehead are small knobs, tiny horns ready to burst through his skin. Five. Five horns.

"I'm almost there. I'm so close to winning. If only I could find the last key," he says, shifting his eyes back to the arcade game.

"Twenty-two. Now serving number twenty-two," the young woman yells from the front desk.

I hurry out the black door and make my way back to the front desk and the woman there. "I'm twenty-two. Uh, what exactly is this place?"

She yawns and then says, "You have three choices. One, be sent back to the house. Two, be sent back to the beginning of the level in which you perished. Three, go back to the point in which you died."

"Where I *died*?"

She turns around, points a remote at a TV mounted behind her and rewinds the video.

"Here it is," she says, replaying my fight with the ghost. I watch myself trying to summon a fireball and then watch the ghost punch me in the stomach. I don't collapse. Instead, I disappear in a puff of smoke.

"Is there any way you can send me back before that?" I ask, waving my hand at the TV.

"That is not an option. At least not on your first death."

"Three then. I choose option three."

She perks up and says, "Now, be advised. I'm required to say this. You'll be in danger of entering a death loop."

"A *death* loop?"

"You may die again, right away. See there." She taps the TV, and it flips. Instead of showing my fight, it shows what's happening right now. Stump and Evie are in the library working their way through the ghost students. "The library where you died is still full of ghosts. If I send you back and you die again you don't have an offering. You'll have no choice but to take my challenge."

"An offering?"

"Yes, an offering. Something to trade. You only get one extra life. Or you can always choose door number four."

"Number four? What's behind it?"

She leans in and whispers, "I'm not supposed to say, but I hear many people talk about a big, bright white light," she says, giggling.

I don't know.

"I'll go with three still," I say.

"Yes, yes. Sorry. Fate humor isn't for everyone. So, before I send you back, would you like to take inventory? Consume any power-ups? Re-charge your spells?"

"Uh, yes," I say.

She picks up an egg timer and hits a button. "You have three minutes."

I swing off Grrblin's pack and kneel to rummage through it. I inspect the Goblin Grub ingredients. An apple, hey, my fireballs. The Wizard Eyes tell me it will give me a fireball. One. It has something to do with its origin.

Next, the nasty green stuff. They'll give me a couple charges of snare. Excellent. Grrblin's sticky bombs might come in handy. None of the other ingredients feel like they'll help.

I pick the monster snot wad (aka ball of sticky green string) out of the pack. The dead horned rat used it to wrap my Wizard Eyes. When I look at the string, it says it has the power to bind magic.

Hmm. I wonder.

I gobble the apple and choke down the nasty green stuff. The last items in the pack are the bottles. My black ones and two orange ones Grrblin didn't use. The black bottles. I don't even want to think about it.

BZZZZZZZ!

"Time's up Number twenty-two. Good luck."

Everything spins like I'm on a terrible carnival ride. And when it stops, I'm standing in the middle of the library next to Stump and Evie.

"Hi," I say.

"Whoa, dude! How'd you come back?"

"Charlie!" Evie says, running up and giving me a monster hug.

"Tell you after we win. Are there any ghosts left?"

"There's one group left in the stacks," Stump says. "We weren't sure how we'd even fight The Angry Librarian after they die."

I dig out the big ball of sticky green string. "I have a plan."

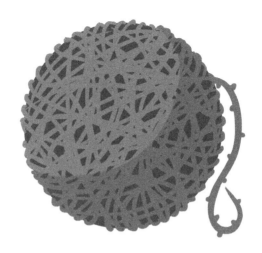

# STICKY STRING

Stump and Evie dash off towards the last few ghosts. They'll wait for my signal.

I'm at the librarian's circular desk wrapping it in sticky green string. Everything I know tells me The Angry Librarian will spawn here. It's her home base.

To be sure it'll do what I want, I wrap the string around the desk three times.

Then I take Grrblin's bow and stash it nearby on a

worktable. I choose one that's close to the desk. On the worktable is a paper the ghosts were working on.

It's math homework. I don't know.

The name on this one is Jesse Rigsby. It sounds familiar. He must spend too much time playing video games and not enough doing his math homework. He's terrible at fractions.

I tug the bowstring back, and an arrow magically appears. Before setting the bow and arrow on the table, I tie sticky green string to the arrow near the feather.

One more thing. I check my pocket. Yup, it's still there. The everlasting gobstopper.

"Beware the klaxon!" I yell.

"AH-OOH-GA!" Stump bellows in return. That means he and Evie are fighting the ghosts.

Listening close, I hear a scream. Oh no.

Evie sprints around the corner and screams, "Run run run. Stump's gone. She's here."

I take off after Evie. "What do you mean she's here?"

"As soon as we poof'd the last ghost, The Angry Librarian popped. She was just there and went right for Stump. Two seconds and he poof'd too."

My plan is already dead. *Think, Charlie*.

"This way," I yell, swinging the opposite direction. We hide in the stacks behind an old dictionary on a pedestal and try to catch our breath.

"What are we going to do now?" Evie asks.

"I want her to chase you."

"You want her to *what*? By myself? Are you crazy?"

"Listen, here's what we'll do," I say, telling Evie the plan.

Evie takes off through the stacks, and I hustle back to the worktable where I stashed the bow and arrow.

It doesn't take long before purple mist blankets the stacks. You can't see anything in there. Evie's footsteps pound the ground and books crash to the floor.

I scan for places Evie might pop out. There. There she is! To the right. Evie flies around a corner and sprints parallel to me. She's waving her hands, and blue sparkles are grabbing books off the shelves and flinging them behind her. The Angry Librarian laughs as the books fall to the floor doing zero damage.

They're almost close enough. One more stack. I pull the everlasting gobstopper from my pocket.

Evie skids around a corner and bolts towards me with the ghost right behind her. The Angry Librarian spots me and stops dead, a scowl crossing her face.

"I'll win. I'll beat you," I say, popping a sticky bomb and catching it. I summon the snare spell, and the baseball-sized thing fills with weeds and vines. They wrap and writhe around my fingers.

The Angry Librarian cracks her jaw. I see the tips of her fangs, yank back my arm, and fling the everlasting gobstopper.

"Evie, now!" I yell. Blue sparkles surround the jawbreaker. Evie makes a forward thrusting motion like she's slamming a door shut. The everlasting gobstopper flies super-fast and super-straight right into the monster's open mouth.

The Angry Librarian looks bewildered, then chuckles, swishing the jawbreaker around in her mouth. She defiantly rolls it between her teeth.

"Bite it, I dare you!" I yell, glaring into those glowing blue eyes. An everlasting gobstopper will last forever. A jawbreaker to rule the world.

The Angry Librarian snarls and bites down.

CRACK!

Her jaw breaks. I launch the sticky bomb, and it hits her right in the chest. The weeds and vines scatter and crawl across her body. She scowls at me and draws breath to scream. But no sound comes. She tries a second time to scream, to steal my magic, but fails. Her jaw hangs loose, she can't make a sound. The Angry Librarian staggers backwards and worry crosses her face.

I laugh.

She bares her claws, and her eyes change, glowing red with rage. She dives towards me, shedding the weeds and vines. I take off running, sprinting for the stacks.

I fly around the shelves of books and make one big loop. The monster picks up speed, getting closer and closer. I can't stay ahead much longer. I turn another corner and Evie is standing on the table with the bow and arrow.

I bolt towards her. Evie draws the arrow, tied with sticky green string, and fires as the monster rounds the corner. The string unwinds through the air. Bullseye! The arrow lodges itself in The Angry Librarian's outstretched clawed hand.

I snatch up the ball of sticky green string and run behind the monster. I chuck the ball to Evie, watching string unwind and wrap around the monster. Evie runs in a half-circle and launches the ball of string to me. Round and round we go. The Angry Librarian spins and dives towards each of us, binding herself in sticky green string like the shoe box my Wizard Eyes came in.

The string runs out, and The Angry Librarian slumps to the ground. She lies on her side and scowls at Evie and I.

I summon my last fireball.

"Game over," I say, and hurl the fireball.

The Angry Librarian explodes into confetti of purple magic. When it clears, I hear a clink. On the ground is a golden key.

It's engraved with the names of our group. It took all of us to get here. It took all of us to win.

A shimmer door appears, and we hop through.

## LOOT LOCKS

I stride into the main room of the house and stand facing the doors. The black one on the left, the white one on the right. Between them is the golden door.

The golden door with seven locks. I inspect the locks. Each is a different size, and some seem connected. One for each of The Seven. The key mobs. The boss mobs.

The golden key from The Angry Librarian fits one

lock perfectly. It turns with a click, and the door creaks open.

Through the door is a tiny room with a single table, holding four magic items. Behind the table is another door with seven locks.

"What the..." I say out loud.

"You expect to beat the game after one boss? You think it'd be that easy?" says a familiar voice.

Turning around, Grrblin has a crazy-big grin on his face.

"Nice job, Eyeball. You did it," he says, slapping me on the shoulder. "After I took one for the team, I figured you guys were toast. Wasn't sure you'd figure things out."

"How many times have you died?" I ask.

"Too many to count. It's a 'video game'. You always come back here to start another room run," Grrblin says with a shrug.

"I didn't come back here. I went to some other place. It was weird. Some kid was playing a game called Magic Eaters, and he had a bunch of bottles of black—"

"No clue, Eyeball. Maybe it's your quest. We'll see, we have time. Lots of time."

Evie and Stump bounce into the room, smiles on their faces.

"Dude, that was awesome!" Stump shouts.

"I couldn't have done it without you guys. Evie

made all the difference," I say, and watch Evie blush. "I'm glad to have friends like you."

"What loot did we get? Magic items? Better be magic items," Stump says, nudging past me to inspect the items on the table.

He picks up a glove which reminds me of the infinity gauntlet. When he slips it on, I notice he doesn't have his basher-arm anymore. He presses a button, and his basher-arm comes back. He presses another button, and his arm morphs again.

"Epic!"

Evie clutches an earring. It's white and looks like a whistle. She inspects it with her Wizard Eyes. "It says fishbone, and it gives me Forever Breath whenever I'm wearing it." She sniffles and rubs her nose.

Grrblin checks the last two items. He picks up the bow. "Better than that crappy one you're using. Which you can keep." He's already replaced his pack, too.

One item left. There's a lump in my throat, and my chest gets tight. It's Mom's gold pen. I peek at it with my Wizard Eyes. Etched into the metal are the words: *use in case of emergency*.

I don't know.

Turning around, my group stares at me. "What?" I say.

"So, what's next?" Evie asks.

I glance at Grrblin, who shakes his head. "Don't look at me."

"Okay, okay," I say, raising my hands. "We'll destroy the key mobs, but we need gear, spells, firepower. Lots of it."

"Now you're talking, dude," Stump says, punching the air.

"I know the place to get it," Grrblin says, grinning.

"But first, where's the rat-man," I say. "Because I hate liars."

## A LITTLE ABOUT
# CONNOR GRAYSON ☆

- Just like Charlie, I got my first gaming console (an NES) after moving across the country. Yes—I bought it with pennies! 😄
- My favorite video games: Super Mario Bros (I can beat the whole game in less than 4 minutes! 😄) and Final Fantasy.
- Two great teachers convinced me to read. (Thank you, Mrs. Lough and Ms. Snyder! 😊) My favorite books: Super Fudge, and Where the Red Fern Grows.
- I was a second baseman in little league, until my all-star's coach moved me to third. ⚾
- If you loved this book, would you tell your teacher about it? Ask them to email me about a virtual visit to your class! 👀
- Find me at ConnorGrayson.com ➡

Made in the USA
Columbia, SC
16 March 2022

57728614R00075